Poems by Young Australians **vol 3**

Random House Australia Pty Ltd
20 Alfred Street, Milsons Point NSW 2061
http://www.randomhouse.com.au

Sydney   New York   Toronto
London   Auckland   Johannesburg

First published by Random House 2005
Copyright © remains with the individual contributors

ISBN 1741660521

Cover and internal illustrations by Bradley Trevor Greive
Cover and internal design by Timothy Clift
Typeset in 10pt Avenir by Aaron Cuneo
Edited by Loretta Barnard
Transcribed by Anita Arnold and Shirley Arnold
Printed and bound by Griffin Press, Netley, South Australia

10 9 8 7 6 5 4 3 2 1

Poems by Young Australians **vol 3**

The best entries from the 2005 Taronga Foundation Poetry Prize

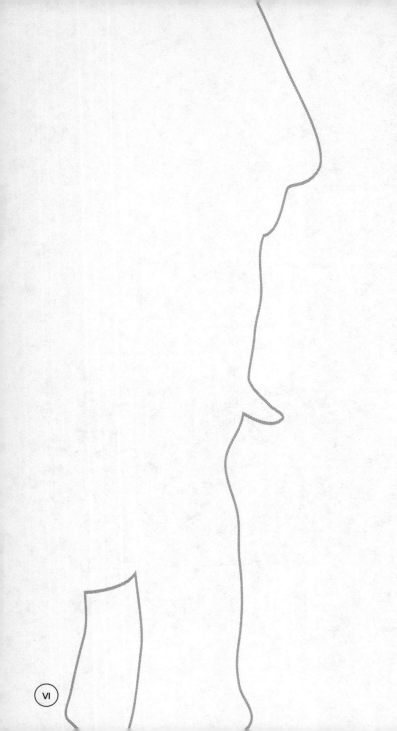

CONTENTS

FOREWORD

'The primary function of poetry, as of all the arts, is to make us more aware of ourselves and the world around us.' (WH Auden, 1938)

Having devoured this delicious anthology, each page a celebration of another year's golden harvest, my eyes stumble over Auden's uncharacteristically dry-mouthed words. It is not for a lesser mind to split hairs with a dead lion, or drag him out of context, though I can't help but think that something important is missing from his irrefutably true statement.

Poetry does create and enhance awareness. Awareness of self, awareness of the other, awareness of place, awareness of the relationships between all three — these qualities are all exquisitely evident within this body of fine poems. But something must always be said for the way in which poetry creates this awareness — the 'magic' of the poem, and I believe it is magic of some sort, for it is quite unlike any other form of creative expression. Whether as mirror or lens, poetry mysteriously turns our eye to something wondrous which was perhaps always there, just not quite in the way we now see it. This poetic phenomenon, however difficult it is to articulate, is as powerful and intangible as gravity itself and is the reason why I, and so many others, will forever love poetry.

I shall further extend my noose-chafed neck by saying there is a unique quality to the best work by young poets. I would not identify this as freshness or rawness *per se*, though these are often present, but more an openness, an honest immediacy that can sometimes be polished away by more schooled poets. You will see exactly what I mean in many of the winning poems in this book, where the journey from heart to page feels as natural and effortless as breath to voice.

That being said, I must quickly add that nobody is born with a platinum pen in their fist. It is no mean feat, however genuine one's love of language, to build a house, a village or indeed a universe with twenty-six letters or less. Crafting a poem may be a labour of love, but it is labour nonetheless. There is seldom a line, stroke or comma that could not be improved with an eraser. That Australian youth have worked so hard in order to carve truth and beauty into parchment makes me feel both inspired and incredibly proud. It remains the greatest privilege to bring this extraordinary talent to your attention.

I sincerely congratulate all poets who entered this year. To have a poem accepted for competition is a tremendous accomplishment in itself. I am sure those luminous few whose work has been published in this volume will know that they have achieved something rare and remarkable. It is pure joy to meet our most talented poets. I note with great pleasure that some of the poets I met at last year's award ceremony are standing on the victory dais again this year — in some cases they have taken new honours in a more senior age group. This is particularly marvellous. I am thrilled to have them back in this anthology, and welcome those who have entered for the first time in 2005. I must say I was particularly impressed this year by the diversity of poetry; the introspection, the powerful and brilliant insights, the sensuality, the vivid extravagance and the humour. That our previous anthologies have won both critical and popular praise, along with a number of publishing awards, speaks volumes for the quality of the work that they contain. In its third year, the Taronga Foundation Poetry Prize has not only maintained its impressive track record, but seems to have come of age. The bar has definitely been raised just a little higher. Entries have risen in both number and quality. This is largely due to the reputation of our noble Director, Professor Ron Pretty AM, the efforts of our tireless Coordinator, Nerida Robinson, and our esteemed judges, who have once again weighed every precious poem with gentle hands and keen eyes.

I am particularly gratified to note that, in a relatively short space of time, our passion for poetry and nature has gathered a great momentum. Thanks to the support of Australia's leading poets and educators, along with many celebrated Australians, such as Richard Morecroft and Libbi Gorr, the Taronga Foundation Poetry Prize has turned heads throughout the country, including that belonging to The Federal Minister for Education, Science and Training, the Hon Dr Brendan Nelson MP, who enthusiastically endorsed the prize by writing to every school in Australia and generously agreed to deliver the keynote address for the 2005 national award ceremony held at Taronga Zoo in Sydney.

Naturally our response to the growing interest in the nation's leading prize for young poets is to expand the prize categories, which now include group/class entries, and to further increase the prize pool. Of course, such growth would not be possible without our key sponsors and supporters. Random House Australia, the Poetry Australia Foundation, Five Islands Press, the University of Wollongong, the University of Melbourne, the Taronga Foundation and BTG Studios all contribute to the success the Taronga Foundation Poetry Prize has become, and which, with their continued support, it will continue to be.

An integral part of the Prize is to offer our entrants a unique and inspiring wildlife experience. This simply would not be possible without the support of Taronga Zoo, Western Plains Zoo, Melbourne Zoo, Weribee Open Range Zoo, Healesville Sanctuary, Australia Zoo, Adelaide Zoo, Monarto Zoo, Perth Zoo, Territory Wildlife Park, National Zoo & Aquarium and Forestry Tasmania. I thank them all for their vision and passion.

As you fall under the spell of our most talented young poets, I suspect you will better appreciate the inspiration that comes from nature. Though almost every conceivable subject is addressed within this anthology, you will be hard pressed to find a poem that is not indebted to nature in some way. A poem is, as with all living things, greater than the sum of its parts. This beautiful literary form is as unique, vital, simple and complex as a flower. The emotional fragility of a lament, for example, comes from its strength as a poem, and the 2005 anthology's Asian elephant motif is intended to highlight this curiously poetic dynamic.

Asian elephants, which are actually more closely related to the woolly mammoth than the African elephant, are now critically endangered. That these mighty creatures have become so vulnerable says much about our world. I am proud that Australian zoo-based conservation groups, particularly Melbourne Zoo, Perth Zoo and Taronga Zoo, are now playing an important role in their recovery through education and breeding programs, awareness campaigns and the contribution of funds and scientific expertise to our conservation partners in Thailand.

I have stood in the shadow of these gentle giants and felt their intelligent gaze upon me. No lover of poetry could ever return unchanged from the presence of a heart so large.

Poetry is life. Life is precious.

Bradley Trevor Greive

Chairman – Taronga Foundation Poetry Prize
Governor – Taronga Foundation

INTRODUCTION

The Taronga Foundation Poetry Prize is now in its third year. From the judges' perspective entries are continuing to grow very strongly, both in terms of the number of poems submitted, which have almost doubled this year, and the overall quality of the poetry, as this volume amply demonstrates.

One of the things that makes the whole process so interesting for us as judges is the range of subject matter these poets are choosing to write about. While, as you might expect, there was some teenage angst from some of the poets, most were able to look beyond themselves to other people and places, and to issues of relevance and interest to their audience.

Another pleasing aspect of the work of these poets was that, as well as writing for themselves – as all poets must – most of them were conscious of the fact that there was a real audience to be written for, to be moved, to be entertained and, in the best poems, to have new light thrown on some aspect of our experience. To come across poems from these young poets that achieved this was genuinely exciting.

As in previous years, we were also struck by the range and sophistication of the verse forms these poets are employing – from sonnets and villanelles to ballads and parodies, visual poems, and the most delicate of lyrics. This range of forms provided us with one of the real pleasures of the judging process, and can be seen reflected in the poems included here.

However, the judges were disappointed that we were unable to award class prizes this year. These were new categories, there were very few entries in them, and the quality is not quite there yet. On the other hand, there were a number of classes where many of the students wrote on much the same subject. An option in these cases would be for the teacher to work with the students to combine their efforts to write a class poem. This provides a great opportunity for students to learn how poetry works from the inside. What's more, it only costs $5 to enter and the prizes come to the school. www.btgstudios.com/worksheet.html has a paper suggesting ways in which teachers might develop poems with their class, so we are hoping for many more entries in these categories next year.

There were again many poems about animals, with lions, cheetahs, kangaroos and Tasmanian devils probably being the most popular. The best animal poems tend to be those where the poets have had a prolonged and direct contact with their subjects. It is more difficult to find something new and fresh to say about a creature that has only been read about, or visited once or twice at the zoo. That perhaps is the reason we did not feel able to award the Wildlife Prize this year. While there were many good and substantial poems dealing with animals and many aspects of the environment, we were unable to find that poem that really stood out from the many others dealing with similar subjects.

On a more positive note, though, there are in this collection of prize-winning and commended poems many to excite and move its readers. Poems of great depth of feeling, poems of close observation (sometimes of things as small and seemingly inconsequential as a shard of china), poems that find new and interesting things to say about relationships between people, linguistically playful poems, parodies, poems that look at commonplace things like, for example, fishbowls from unusual perspectives. There are poems that explore the world from a range of religious or spiritual perspectives, and others that explore what it feels like to be bullied. There are poems that explore myths, more than one of which reminded me of AD Hope's lines in 'An Epistle from Holofernes':

> …the myths will not fit us ready-made.
> It is the meaning of the poet's trade
> To recreate the fables and revive
> In men the energy by which they live…

There are delicate webs of words, and robust frolics and carefully controlled sonnets and striking visual poems and humour and reminiscence and the continued delight of turning the next page. The judges commend these poets, as well as the many fine poets who didn't quite make it this time, and look forward with much anticipation to next year's offering.

Ron Pretty AM

Director – Taronga Foundation Poetry Prize
Director – Poetry Australia Foundation

POEMS

'A king brown on the rotten floor. We ran for our lives, my brother and I ...'

JESSE LUKE LOVERIDGE

Hurry & Hustle

"Hurry, Hurry get up quick
    it's time for us to go.
Eat your corn-flakes, pack your bag,
    why must you be so slow?"
Now that's my Mum, going on at me...
    to get me on my way;
To rush to school all neatly dressed,
    to start another day.

"Hurry, hurry what have you done? What
    answer did you get?
WHAT, still on question twenty-one? You
    haven't finished yet?"
Now that's my teacher pushing me, to
    do Mathematics.
Of course I'll get my sums all right, but
    better do it quick!

"Hurry, hurry get there fast, you've
    got to take this catch.
Come on Jessie, move it Jess, we
    want to win this match."
They're my team mates cheering me, to
    GO, GO, GO and GO.
Of course I'm going to catch the ball, what
    makes them think I'm slow?

"Hurry Jess, Hurry up; are you
   still in the shower?
It's ages since you went in there, must
   you take an hour?"
It's father's turn to hassle me, to
   hurry things along
It's only church we're going to; it's
   ONLY EVENSONG!

All day long and every day, we're
   rushing, so it seems.
No time to look, no time to think, no
   time for any Dreams!
What's the point of charging in, to do
   it "Oh! So Fast."
She _lives_ the most, she _sees_ the best,
   the one who strolls in last.

My Farm

Between afternoon and night
Fishing with my fishing rod,
Catching fish for dinner.
Running through the mud,
Climbing the sloping hills,
Gumboots sloshing while I run.
Mum, my brothers and me.

Snake in the rusty old truck.
Under the big fig tree.
A king brown on the rotten floor.
We ran for our lives, my brother and I,
Hearts pumping hard,
Legs bolting up the driveway,
Screaming for our mum.

In the dead of night.
A pack of dingoes hunting for food.
Attacked our cow,
Biting and scratching and jumping
In the morning, only one dingo left.
The dead cow on the ground.
We left it there.

A peaceful place.
Old wooden farm house.
Original dairy still standing.
Cattle-yards near the barn.
Swimming pool for fun.
This is my farm.

The War

There's silence tonight in the darkness
No dogs bark and no one calls out.
Smoke drifts up from the Valley
And far off in the distance someone shouts.

We lie close to keep out the night's cold
Beside me my father lies asleep
But my mother is wide-awake
Too scared to even weep.

The war came for no real reason
The anger in somebody's head.
He led his team to our village
3 days and we were dead.

There was blood outside the garden
Where me and Michael used to play
Where my dog used to lie in the sunshine
Where my parents sat every day.

I stare out in the darkness
The stars and the moon are still there
And the sun comes up every morning
But the happiness has gone from the air.

The grass keeps on growing
And the fields are filled with corn
Which was put with the dead of our village
Who were buried at dawn.

Figures move down in the valley
Setting the houses alight
Killing the last of our families
Tearing the heart out of night.

A dog came yesterday evening
Collapsed at the mouth of the cave
It shivered with every gunshot
Like us, too scared to be brave.

Last Saturday I was eleven
Now too old to be young
My childhood died with Michael
There are no more songs to be sung.

4 years old, too young to die
He lay in the sandpit
We thought all hope was lost
After that terrible hit

We buried him under the big tree
Where generations were hid from the sun
Such a tall, beautiful mountain
Where songs seemed to be sung

How can there be god up in heaven
When people are killed every day,
People too old to walk
Babies too young to pray

Far away in the world
People send us a prayer
Throw dollars into a bucket
To pretend that they care

The photos move through the paper
From headlines and then page 3
Then back past the shares and the cricket
And to what's on T.V.

And when I am old and past caring
About all the worries of life
I'll still see Michael's body
Saved from a lifetime of strife

Will time travel backwards?
Will the birds come back to the sky?
Will any thing be any better?
Will we be able to cry?

And will our lives become easy
Free from depression and pain?
Of course not, but now the others
Will come with a different name

Billycart Blues

Tho' Chester was an average kid he didn't have a clue
Red hair and heaps of freckles, his mates all called him Blue
While Blue was quite mischievous his capers all showed heart
But nothing quite compared to when he made a billycart.

It started when he found out back some old wheels off a pram
A light inside his head switched on and then it all began
He gathered up some bits of wood, some nails and then some screws
And tho' he'd not made one before, what did he have to lose?

Blue put that thing together a little hastily
Assembly in the shortest time was a necessity
To say he was an ideas man would not have been untrue
But did I neglect to mention that he didn't have a clue?

Blue couldn't wait a moment more to try his billycart
The top of Deadman's Hill he found a perfect place to start
At nigh a hundred miles an hour he'd really raised the stakes
But then in horror realised that he'd forgot the brakes!

Now at the base of Deadman's Hill an old shed filled with hay
At least Blue hoped it was still there – it was the other day
'Twas with a huge sigh of relief the shed came into sight
But Blue just couldn't seem to steer – he'd gotten such a fright.

Blue's speedy new contraption sailed right on past that shed
And plunged down twenty metres into the creek instead
Blue learned from this experience – despite not being smart
And now he gets his buddies to test drive his billycarts!

Extinct

They stare reproachfully,
Those silent watchers, whispering their story in
Forests that are no longer there.

Hidden from view,
Megafauna march sombrely through
Suburban streets,
Shades of a former age,
As the urban population of ghosts
Grows, swelling the ranks of the
Plaintiffs who walk our cities and appear in
None of our courts.

The lost ones perch on roofs and
Stalk through avenues scarcely
Reminiscent of shaded paths,
Where the dappled luminance of trees has
Disappeared, replaced by motorists speeding by,
Unseeing and unseen by those that,
Though lost forever,
Cry from beyond gloomy graves,
"Hold, hold"...

Gloucester Cathedral

We visited Gloucester Cathedral.
Feeling very irreverent,
Walking through the great, grand doors,
Two giggling eighteen year old atheists.
Walked through the Cloisters,
Where the tombs of the famous and forgotten
Are paving stones.
Looked at architecturally significant windows
(Not knowing the name of the style)
And did Harry Potter impressions,
Whispering, "Snape's coming to get me"
And using a mobile phone as a wand
And took a photo.
We stroll past a sign saying,
"Quiet please, exams in progress"
And laugh at the poor sufferers
Stuck in a hot room doing what we finished
Forever, six months ago.

Past grand tombs
With white marble statues of men and women
Lying in Great Majesty,
Not sure whether they're more freaky or fascinating.
Stare at an odd table we realise is a mirror
Reflecting the roof above
Which is fabulously ornate.
It is cold, as all churches are
With uneven flagstone flooring
And that mouldy smell of antiquity
Which is suggestive of museums,
Underground tunnels and catacombs,
A seriousness so profound,
No unbeliever will ever understand it.
We light a candle and tip in some spare pennies
Gouged from the bottom of my bag
Amidst the lint and lolly wrappers.
Try to think of a prayer for the congregation
But decide it is too rude
To offer up a prayer for people who don't pray.
For an atheist I have a great fear
Of showing disrespect in church,
I don't get it enough to knock it,
Whatever I may say outside.
We walk down the aisle to an
Imagined Wedding March
Trying to pretend no one's looking,
Pick up a brochure (in French)
To prove we've been to
This dignified, beautiful
Tourist attraction.
Step out into the sunshine and head for the bus and
for home.

The Remnant

It is smooth inside my hand
the china curving softly
'til it meets
the jagged edge of brokenness.

I smooth the softened soil
from its side
a pale brown smudge
remaining
like an afterthought.

How long has this remnant lain in the earth
beneath the broken down house in the bush?

How many words
of love
laughter
loss
were shared
over tea drunk from this cup?

Was this a lonely bride's only company
her husband a drover
riding horseback
far away?

Was this her mother's
tearful last gift
her lips tight
with holding back tears
as she kisses her daughter goodbye
leaving England
for an unseen land?

Was this her children's cup
as they played at tea parties
with water from the creek?

Did it break in anger,
an argument
thrown against the wall?

Or carelessness
her tears slipping down its
smooth white curves
as she looked at the pieces in her hand?

Or was it just forgotten
left outside in the rain
as small feet raced inside from play?

And am I somehow connected with her
over the unbroken stretch of time
for finding it
lost and forgotten.

A remnant
of a life
long since lived.

The Day My Creativity Left Me

In year twelve maths
Problems were being hammered into my head.
Bell went, next lesson.
Chemical terms were being repeated, learnt, revised.
In Classics every character's action was picked apart
Until personality and spontaneity were but an equation
Or a plot tool.
And it was at that point
My head kicked my creativity clean out!
Stunned at first, it sat at my feet
And though I realised its place and injury
I had no time to pick it up.
Realising it was unloved it shed a tear.
And it up
And it left
And I never saw it again.
I miss it more than any limb or sense –
My outlet, my passion, my potential.
The cost of learning Pythagoras
Is high these days.

'My feet are tangled up in grass still wet from last night's dew and I am like a pharaoh embalmed in his own skin.'

MICHAEL MALAY

Born Too Soon

Baby boy, born too soon
Welcome to the world four months early.
Fighting for life,
Fragile,
Frail,
Tiny.

Baby boy, born too soon
Welcome to Intensive Care.
Machines,
Doctors,
Drugs,
Pain.

Baby boy, born too soon
Welcome to medical issues.
Chronic Lung Disease,
Brain haemorrhages,
Retinopathy,
Seizures.

Baby boy, born too soon
Welcome to the world!
Tenacious,
Stubborn,
Survivor,
Me.

I am

I am happy the way I am.
I am a ten-year-old girl,
I think of myself
As absolutely fine.
I am happy the way I am!

I am the roar of the waves,
I am as ugly as wolf.
I am the sound of the cello,
I am as pretty as flower.
Who will understand,
I am happy the way I am!

I am a high mountain,
I am as happy as puppy.
I am the bottom of a muddy creek,
I am as furious as an ogre.
Who will understand,
I am happy the way I am!

I will not change,
I will stay the same.
Who will understand,
I am happy the way I am!

The Sad Sonnet of a Bullied Boy

On the porch, across the upturned chair,
    The boy would spread a striped counterpane,
Against the length and gloom of the rain,
    And on all fours crawl under it like a bear.
To mend his wounds in secret, in his lair,
    And afterwards, in the windy yard again,
One hand cocked back to release his paper plane.
    Frail as a twig into the faithless air.
Summer evenings he would whirl around,
    Faster and faster till the drunken ground
Rose up to meet him; sometimes he would squat
    Among the bent weeds of the vacant lot,
Waiting for dusk and someone dear to come,
    To gently lead him to his haven home.

The photo

I'd like to think it always
stayed the same as it was then
Sam in his blue baby suit and his sandy hair fine
flat on his chubby head
Me absorbed in a dreamy sleep
lips pouted and red
our heads resting on each other
no eyebrows and blank expressions
    no worries
    or responsibilities
    just babies asleep.

The photo is framed
    light wood
    but solid
an oval shape for never-ending
    if only it was
    babies forever
Mum is grinning with pride
the doctor smirking in the corner
Dad trying to hush the nurse's "Ooow's".

Nearly 14 years ago
on a soft white blanket
my twin brother and I
slept
with no worries
or sad thoughts
but were peaceful
unaware there was anything else.

Babies asleep.

If only it stayed the same
being babies,
minds unaware.

Akimbo (I would speculate)

I would speculate

that i am pretty t o g e t h er
most of the time
    so what is the time now?
i would check
    but i do not own a watch.
actually, there are a lot of things that i do not own
though there are so many things that i possess
i possess my own thoughts
they are wholly mine
    not always holey
        sometimes h o ley
though nevertheless...

                    mine.
my brain consists of thoughts
piled on top of each other
                        layer
                            upon
                                layer
just like a cake
except that the thoughts are not always sweet
sometimes they are so bitter
that i scrape my head
to get rid of the taste.

but i can't get rid of it.

just like i can't get the smell of these cigars
out from underneath my fingernails
just like i can't erase the notion of you
i scrub till my skin is flamingo raw
but you remain
                        Imprinted
                                in my cerebellum.

i hope you are proud

give yourself a pat on the back

you dilettante.

***

you are such a holey person
that I am scared
that one day
all your substances
will abandon you
and fall through a hole
on the side of your hip

You will be left empty
but do not feel frightened
because I will feed you
and fill you
and kiss your pepper sores
I will mend you
and fix you
and sew you back up

I am not emotic
Or extrovertly romantic
I am volatile
though essentially

I prefer empathy to sympathy
and if all the sensations
you have the ability to feel
are dry
then I'll cut out half of mine
and present them to you
I do not have much
though that is everything I can offer you

So
have half of me
and we can walk around
as half-people
but more whole now
Believe me
take my half
and
you will never be holey again.

The Death of Hecuba

They're all gone now.
What's left?
The beach is scarred.
Too much fire.
Too much death.
This is where they laid my son.
Where they dragged his body.
Where we buried him.
Where they killed my daughter.
Where her blood fell.
Where they kept the knife.
Where they laid my grandson.
Where his mother's tears fell.
Where he is buried.
This is my city.
Where my children were born.
Where they killed them.
Where they butchered my husband.
Where they laid him to die.
Where I wept for him.
This is where the gods walked.
Where the heroes were.
Where they did
Their grand deeds.

Star-Crossed Lovers – the real story

Permit me to recount this sordid story
Full of details, gross and gory.
Of Romeus and his sire's vendetta,
Against the family of fair Julietta.
A lovely girl, with beauty's grace,
Of sweet demeanour and youthful face,
Youthful – for her and her peers
Had not yet witnessed fourteen years.

They spent their moments chatting gaily,
Smiling sweetly, shopping daily,
Beguiling cash from their doting dads,
To finance all their yuppie fads.
These were the girls of fame and money,
Julietta was queen, the reigning honey.

By contrast, on the other side of town
Was where Romeus lay his head down.
The streets were dirty, the dwellings crude,
The dogs were mangy, the people rude.

Among them all strode Montague,
A businessman... and a crook too.
He'd educate his love-sick son:
"Romeus, you'll only have won
In life if you can safely say
That all the money comes your way.
Forget the girls, you don't need a wife
To succeed and to enjoy your life.

My son, just pay your heed to me
And you'll never endure celibacy,
Just lots of assets, lots of cash
That attracts the girls, both shy and brash
Who'll offer their whole selves to you,
Take... but give no brass razoo.
The only reason they share their honey
Is so they can take your hard earned money!

Work hard, but swindle even harder!
Buy some stocks! Learn to barter!
Watch the markets every day!
Then my son... you'll be ok.
To you my fortune I will leave,
So when I die you needn't grieve,
But before I will you all my money,
You have to do something for <u>me</u> sonny.

NEVER MARRY! Heavens above!
Let BUSINESS be your only love!
Don't be trusting any man,
Count your drachmas, every dram,
Do NOT show folks you're rich as hell,
Of your great wealth, never tell.

The final lesson, 'fore you inherit,
Is my hatred for old Capulet.
That old man once worked for me
Filing papers; then you see,
He stole some millions, embezzling swine,
Then went bought some real cheap wine,
Sold it at a massive profit,
Now he's living nicely off it!

And here's the part that's really vile,
The tenacity! It raises my bile,
The townsfolk think he's innocent,
And I'm the one they think is bent!!

That fable of inheritance
From rich rellies who lived in France
Fooled everyone, BUT DID NOT FOOL ME!
So my son, do you now see,
The day you link our names, I fear,
You will be out! Right on your rear,
BANISHED! From my heart and mind,
So I hope I never ever find
That you, my son, have shamed my name,
Tarnished it with Capulet's dame."

While Romeus heard his dad's vendetta,
Capulet's dame, young Julietta,
Was in an agitated state,
For Prince had asked her on a date!
Bobby Prince went to her school,
And was considered uber-cool.
(Even a princess like Julietta,
Could not have done very much better.)

With her outfit she was getting fluster'd:
The red dress all wrong, as was the custard
Top with her new denim jeans,
Oh! Fashion was so hard for teens!

She finally chose a dress of blue
And made up her face with some goo,

Put a ribbon in her hair,
Then while she was sitting there,
The doorbell rang, loud, alarming,
"Oh, that must be my own Prince Charming"
And with that witty interjection,
Pucker'd up, kissed her reflection,
And went to meet her Prince at last,
Leaving lipstick on the glass.

The movie was slow, the movie was boring,
A baby was crying, a fat old man snoring,
Julietta yawned, voluntarily shook
With cold, gave Prince a piercing look
When he noticed not and gave her no arm
To warm her and soothe with his comforting palm.

The movie was frankly, disgustingly crude,
And Bobby was being frightfully rude!
He'd bought himself popcorn, not offered her any,
(not that she craved, calories it had many).
He picked the movie "ALIEN BAIT"
Julie sighed, it wasn't much of a date.
She'd imagined kissing and love everlasting,
Not flesh-eating monsters and alien blasting!

Just when Julie was feeling quite vile,
She noticed a _somebody_ just down the aisle,
A quite handsome lad, she'd seen him at school –
But she'd always thought him rather a fool,
He spent all his school days sat in detention,
That is, when he wasn't away on suspension!

She'd never really liked Romeus before
But shown Prince's real side, she now liked him
   much more.
She knew Rome did things like drinking and fighting,
Her dad hated his dad, it made him exciting...

Quite soon after they were the school power pair,
Romeus and Julietta, one dark and one fair,
Making out in the playground and during class,
But Rome's friends said Julie was a pain in the a**!
She made Romeus sissy Mercutio reckoned,
A boytoy, a lapdog, he came when she beckoned.

Romeus wouldn't listen to his friend's lies,
He had Julie in his hands and stars in his eyes!
He'd never been in love with a girl so fine
(That is, since he had broken up with ex Rosaline.)
For three whole days he'd been broken-hearted,
Since with his dear Rosaline he had parted,
Then to the movies he went in a fateful decision,
There Cupid had truly struck with precision!

Never was there such a pure love as this,
I mean, Julie even knew how to French kiss!
He daydreamed about her, she smiled as she slept,
When one night she stealthily out of her house crept,
And went to a party with her darling Rome,
Since then she was hardly ever home!

She used to be sweet and loving to her dad,
Now she got moody and was rather bad,
She drank and she smoked and she tried every drug,

Where once was a sweetheart, there now was a thug.
She stole from charities she used to collect for,
She swore and skipped school, she was bad to the core.

But one thing that stayed the same throughout,
Was her love for Romeus, that girl-changing clout,
He'd corrupted her thoroughly, outside and in,
She started thinking herself fat, threw up to get thin.

And this is the climax of the story,
Where starts the details gross and gory,
For although Julietta used to be nice,
She now was engaged in every kind of vice,
(Even the ones which are ill-fated,
They can't be mentioned as they aren't PG rated),
But still she was pretty, just frightfully thin,
And Bobby Prince still loved her, she just didn't love him.
She idolised Romeus, loved him blindly,
He was the only one she now treated kindly.

When one dark night, rain, thunder and lightning,
Lit up the skies, it was rather frightening,
But not to Romeus and Julietta,
Who thought a night could not have been better,
For kissing and touching and driving and drinking
All at once, the poor kids cannot have been thinking.

The alcohol must have been rationale impeding,
For Romeus, driving, was dangerously speeding
Along a curvy range, slippery with rain.
The lightning flashed once, it then flashed again.
And it found Rome's body laid out in the mud,
His beautiful body... all covered in blood.

For Romeus was thrown when the car overturned,
The image of his dead body forever burned
In his beloved girlfriend Julietta's brain,
As his blood washed away in the torrents of rain.
She cried for herself, for Romeus, this sad scene,
Her whole life ruined, before she was fourteen.

At Romeus' funeral, Julietta cried,
She wished she was gone too, she thought of suicide,
Together forever in the vast afterlife,
She'd be with Romeus, his eternal wife,
But when she tried to, literally, kill her pain,
She shook, she just couldn't face death again.

She became quiet, withdrawn, confined to her bed,
The horrible scene replayed in her head,
Over and over, a horrible dream,
Romeus' body, Romeus' scream...

Eventually, with help, she returned to school
And it was as if Julietta was new,
A new person, no longer bad to the bone,
No swearing, and drinking, talking hours on the phone...

She was a bit quiet, she was kind of shy,
No longer evil, no longer sly,
For Romeus had been the one to cause her bad side,
For him she had her dad's rules defied,
But he had not been all bad, now she knew clearly,
He'd been her first love, her best love, he'd loved
  her sincerely.

Julie thought she'd never get over this phase,
But as Dad said, *"Love works in mysterious ways..."*
One day in the library she met Bobby Prince's big
  brother,
He was smart, he was funny, he was kind to his mother.
Physically, he had everything Romeus had got,
But Romeus, Adam Prince definitely was NOT.

They started to go out, Julie's heart started to mend,
But that didn't mean she forgot her first boyfriend.
Romeus had been a big part of her life,
But that didn't stop her becoming Adam's wife.
Years later, with her children upon Adam's knee,
Julietta still grieved at Romeus' stupidity.

There is a moral to this tale,
That is if you are young and male,
You shouldn't drive your car drunk or fast,
Or else your life just might not last.
And even your sweet femme fatale,
Your Venus, your own special gal,
Will not lay down her life for you,
She'll cry, then marry a Prince too.

Three

I – Waiting

Circe:
Here on the shore I wait
I don't understand him
Come and then gone.
As though I shouldn't feel,
Shouldn't cry as the boat went out.
As though it didn't matter,
Didn't matter that I was alone.
Here on the shore I wait.

Calypso:
Here in the cave I wait
He said he loved me
But he is gone.
As though I was meant to accept it,
As though it didn't matter,
But he cried and I forgave him,
He cried and it seemed alright.
Here in the cave I wait.

Penelope:
Here by the tapestry I wait
Twenty years and one hundred threads:
But he is still gone.
As though I could perfectly manage,
As though it never hurt.
As though my tears were water,
His absence bringing forth only rain,
Here by the tapestry I wait.

II – Questions

Circe:
What will he say of me?
What will he tell the listeners?
What will they make of me?
Will they say I'm a witch?
Will they understand?
What will he say of me?

Calypso:
What will he think of me?
What will he ponder at night?
When will he turn to me?
Will he ever come back in thought?
Will he wish for me in his arms?
What will he think of me?

Penelope:
Where does he stand at this moment?
Does he think of his home?
Will he be happy forever on some foreign shore?
Are the rumours true?
Does he really love her?
Where does he stand at this moment?

III – Later

Circe:
One year and two children later,
What did he say to me?
Why not stay forever?
Why not be free?
No he leaves forever,
Leaves for the path home,
One year and two children later.

Calypso:
Seven years and a shipwreck later,
What did he want from me?
Was I the one he loved?
Was this the place for him?
No I'm still the extra,
He can depart free,
Seven years and a shipwreck later.

Penelope:
Twenty years and a slaughter later,
How did he appear,
In love or war and hatred?
What did he say at the end?
Only that he still loves me,
As though nothing's changed,
As though it's all alright:
Twenty years and a slaughter later.

Timothy's Dad

Timothy, your father left while you were at school.
When did he leave?
About five minutes from inevitable o'clock
But only time truly knows

Timothy, your father left while you were at school.
How did he leave?
He was anger itself in the form of someone we loved
But only time saw properly

Timothy, your father left while you were at school.
Why did he leave?
Factors include: depression, arguments and endurance;
Please check the list to see if you made the team
But only time is psychic

Timothy, your father left while you were at school.
What about his job?
Your father never was one to think of money first
But time may be taking his shift

Timothy, your father left while you were at school.
When is he coming back?
When the world is reborn to a time of predictable beings
But only time will tell

Timothy, your father left while you were at school.
I thought he loved us?
I loved him for 13 years and you loved him for 10
but time makes fools of us all

Timothy, your father left while you were at school.
Is he coming back at all?
There are some things nobody is meant to know
Not even time itself....

Family Shrine

I remember walking with my parents
bearing plastic bags filled with apples and oranges,
respects for my father's father and mother,
the grandparents I never knew.

We walked past a news-stand,
a shabby noodle shop, a convenience store,
clothes boutiques galore –
an unlikely location, I thought.

A dim arcade, stony-cold and closed in,
a musty, faltering lift reluctantly took us to
I don't remember what floor.
Above the traffic, behind several doors,

my grandparents' portraits among an array
of faces, a collage covering an entire wall,
black and white fading to brown,
each face individual, looking over us.

We offered our fruit at this communal shrine,
kneeling down on the velvety red cushions,
waving smoking incense sticks in rhythm
with muttered prayers, then bowing three times.

On the other side of the room
stood a statue of Guanyin, the Bodhisattva.
For good measure we planted some incense sticks
in her ashy bowl.

***

A robed monk sits by the window on a vinyl bench,
eyes closed, mouth moving, long fingers
swiftly brushing beads
along a thread

click,
click,
click.

Requiem for a Pope

Written on the night before the death of
Pope John Paul II

Tonight is your last, messenger,
and though life seeps
away, gently
can you hear them whispering?

We are all from stars, brother
     stardust.   Duller
     the light fades
     your light fades
falling in upon yourself.

Where is it you're looking?
     Is it to the masses?
And though their eyes are on you
they can not carry you, nor follow you
     leader.   Your book
bound tight, does it tell you
of the next place, can you see it, reader?

If tonight be your last, messenger,
   and when you feel
the last grains slip through
the narrow necked gate
   listen for the voices! Can you hear your brothers?
Look for the brightness, have no fear!

But when you hear none,
see none
feel none
are none, tell me brother

where is your God if not here.

Juniper Burning

(Early in the mornings, Tibetan monks burn handfuls of juniper to stave off bad weather. The resulting white smoke is also used as an offering to the spirits.)

He is awake early. Rising before the others.
Morning light glancing off his shaved head
then falling into his mouth
like slow mango milk.

From finger to shoulder his skin runs naked
and running naked, climbs in long brown stretches
   up his forearm
erupting suddenly into thick saffron layers, where it
   falls over his shoulders
plunges down to the heel
everything but his arms covered beneath cloth
   and tradition.
This robe once worn by his father.

He is 19. Slender. Standing at the juniper tree
this his most private pleasure of the morning
where the senses stagger, crack, fall
– eliminating thought
touch of leaf against him, his nose swallowing
whatever it can touch.
The empty courtyard.

He is moving up the steps now. Climbing the high
walls overlooking the temple.
His robe slipping over stone, disrupting pebbles
from sleep.

Though at the top of the climb
there is always that moment, he knows,
where his hand sweeps across the fire
dropping things
heat curling around the juniper branch
like a mad bird's wing.

Today, if there is no rain, they will meditate outside.

Missing you

I was harvesting poetry from old drawers,
Sitting on my comforting throne of yellowed papers, while
Earth laid low in the cool of night, and the house was dark,
Breathing slow, and deeply
Snoring.

I found an old poem: "Missing you", and read it,
   laughing silently
At childish lavishness; sugar cliché,
And chiding myself for the overuse
Of words like "ache" and "despair"...
I would never write anything like that now.
I would simply remind you of the things
That I probably once would have said.

Do you remember the way we watched each other?
Do you remember the way we were aware of each other?
There was that warm mantle around our shoulders, and
Beneath it we huddled, like small feathered things.
My hair was dark and yours pale like moonlight
Mingling down our backs, and you were the one I pressed
Up against me and held close,
And I hoped you would never need to leave me.

At morning, as the earth turned warm in the mouth of the sun,
I crawled back to bed, clutching air that was the shape of you,
And prayed, slowly, to dream of us, together;
Pausing a long time on each   of the
Words.

greatest loss

this future shifts out of focus when
the lens begins to thicken but i'd have thought
i wouldn't need vision in this familiar place – thought
off-by-heart could answer any questions as i felt my way
in the dark. but who would have known fingertips could
grow numb over time? i can't feel you like
i used to. can't feel our history in my veins, pulsing
into memory whenever i see you (however distant).

i thought the attrition into numbness would have been clearer or
predictable, like the trains they speak of, rushing through
tunnels long seconds after we hear them coming (turn our heads
to catch the rush of wind we know is to follow). thought i'd get
that pins and needles tingling that precedes paralysis or my
    circulation
being cut off (trapping the blood so i can't feel you creeping up
    behind me).

my divination can no longer sense you – out
of my range or just flying too low for my radar to
capture. can't take your hands without wondering, 'what
have my fingers disappeared into? these folds of skin
can't be real, my flesh can't make contact (no
contact without sensation).' what have i lost? i think about

what i have lost. i have lost nothing
but feeling. i have lost nothing

but you.

WINNER SENIOR

Chris Summers | AGE 17 NSW

For Vitaliy

I take his hand.

My fingers caress his
Leather palm, tracing the
Tapestry of
Deep, intricate lines.
Dry.

His nails are dirty yellow
Stained
But smooth,
Well-kept.

I hold it.

I softly knead
The sagging,
Supple flesh, feeling
Stones beneath my thumbs.
Knuckles hard, obtrusive, buried
In rolls of skin
Laid thick.

I let go.

And I explore.

I know his face like a dog-eared book.

My fingers dance and
Spring across his
Swollen cheeks,
Rich, red.

They climb through
Creases, scale
The furrowed folds
Of his brow.

They wander through grey
Tufts of hair,
Thin and wispy
Here and there, then
Gently brush his eyes;
Steel blue and
Wide awake.

He beams; thin lips
Wrinkle,
Stretch and curve
Around his face.

A full smile, and
I smile too.

I take his hand.

I know his face like a dog-eared book.

I want to know

Though never have
We touched,
Heard a laugh,
A voice.

Who are you?

Only ever
Sterile, safe
Words uttered in passing,
Mumbled or whispered.

Who are you?

Never more
Than lifeless photos
Flat, tainted
By time.
Decrepit,
Worn and loved.

Who are you?
I have never known,
Never shared more
Than blood.

I let go.

But blood is thick.
And somehow,
I feel.

Paradise Point Blues

Tired of reading the French poets
I go outside
to lean against the silence –
of a thick winter morning.

Birds assault the sun
                    throwing their bodies
            into the air

            strange
            this choreography of the sky.

My feet are tangled up in grass
still wet
from last night's dew
and I am like a pharaoh
embalmed in his own skin.

This is what I look at:
the lawn
my neighbour's fence
and the garden gnome
– missing its left ear

I stand with my coffee
and smudge my toes
                    into the ground.

This is when my mind starts running
when I remember useless facts:
the various fish of South Australia
the year Alexander the Great
– destroyed Persepolis
the time you said
tea should be brewed
for 2 minutes exactly.

On mornings such as this
we had rainy quick conversation
as we washed breakfast plates
and waited for the grass to dry.

On mornings such as this
Miles Davis was crying
being all dizzy and sad
in the background

Up-beat trumpet
beat-up soul
gramophone

I laughed
when you tried
to say something
in Spanish
unable to pronounce the double 'l'
you said something quite rude
but I forgave you.

I told you
          I wanted to go
                    some place
                              as far flung
                    as New York
so I could speak in accents all day
and pretend to be Irish.

You told me
the best thing to do
was to be drunk and fall asleep
and I'd be Irish anyway.

On mornings such as this
we'd exchange dreams
and eat pancakes.

You had one
where an elephant
                    went to the Vatican
                    had tea with the Pope
                    and played golf with his cardinals.

In mine
the world got drunk
and everyone was being serenaded
by pigs blowing whistles
in barnyards gone mad.

We laughed at these strange things
and loved these strange things in ourselves.

Once
the grass was being trampled
by curious birds
writing
footprint stories
in silver snow grass

You would look at this
                              and tell me

that a bird's foot was lighter than a match
or that the beating heart of a sparrow
ticks faster than we can count.

And as in a dream
we would speak slowly
our fingers pointing at the sky
and her crazy clouds.

We shared things of each other
and stole things from each other
held things so tightly they smashed
scaring the embarrassed birds away.

Funny
      how a garden gnome
           can make you feel
                so sad.

Standing here
I smudge my toes
           into the ground
              drawing lines like Picasso

I'm in this broken coat
the one that you so famously bought
off a gypsy
in Madrid.

And suddenly my mind's been caught
by this laughing bleeding image
                of a man
                on a balcony
                alone, drunk

pretending to be an Irishman
                in New York.

The coffee has burnt my tongue
all birds have delicate feet.

I go back inside
and read a book.

Roll Call at Bondi Beach (Roll of Honour)

R.Burns.P.Baird
J.Clements.R.Clifton
S.Anderson.W.Dawson
J.Clements.V.DavisB.Evans
C.J.Cockayne.R.H.Dougherty.A.A.Fyfe
A.DunfordC.DunlopW.Gaskell
T.Dwyer.J.GoschD.Impey
C.A.Freestone R.Geldart
R.HannabyA.Hurlock
G.NoakesA.Neilson
C.IrvineJ.F.Mills
W.Kerr.G.Kolb
J.Lockyer
Lockhead
B.A.McDonald.R.Mayberry.H.E.McDonald
A.McGavin.E.Norwood.P.O'Connor.L.J.O'Kane
G.E.S.Valli.Pearce.R.C.Russell.H.SaundersR.A.Taylor
I.R.Stephenson.V.R.Thomas.M.A.Treacy.G.Thompson
J.S.Attard J.HTruscott.N..Wallwork.L.Allen R.Barrett
F.Bryant R.M..Woolhouse.W.G.Boddington D.Carland
W.Carhill Bell.B.F.Carlson.A.J.ClareW.Clark J.I.Dawson
A.I.Cook W.P.Cox.J.Craig.L.Croton.G.Crump L.W.Cook
A.J.Davis L.D.DeeleyF.A.Dolphin.T.F.Doolan S.C.Ellery
L.Edwards J.JH..Egan.G.R.Etty.R.A.Farnsworth I.Edwards
T.Fletcher J.Ferguson.G.Gibson.P.Gill.A.Gosch C.I.Follett
M.Greenwood.T.Hall.R.Hamilton.W.G.Hanock.E.A.Harris.JW.Haywood.Cook.A.T.Hayes
Roll of Honour F.Key R.V.Hunter.S.R.Hunter.A.E.Jackson
Owen Stanley Mountains+ +R.L.Kelton
J.Harvey.G.W.Tindell.A.W.Pottinger **Gona** A.Key
E.A.Lowe.C.R.McCallum.S.Mc.Clure
Mc **On the Kokoda Trail** Intosh
J.McDonald.C.M.McGillivary
A.I.McPherson.J.M.Matthews
J.A.Metson.A.J.Misson.C.Nye
C.G.Moffatt.PMoltoni.S.Oppy
G.G.Moore.J.Moore.R.Morris
J.Nelson.M.Nisbet.W..Noble
F.J.Noonan.T.Parish.H.Salter
J.P.O'Sullivan.W..Ratchford
E.A.Randall.N.W.Smethurst
C.H.Roberts, G.L.Speechley
N.Spooner.D.Smith.J.Smith
J.P.Scullion.D.SmithB.Stead
T.Snelgar.A.Souter.C.R.Tice
G.I.Spokes.A.Taylor.L.Veale
E.G.Vial.L. Waller.A.Warn
H.Warman R.Watt.D.Wills
Wilkinson D.G.T.Wilson
B.Thomas J.A.Whellans
Horwood S.D.Johnston
Munro Mayne
I.Leask E.Lowe
E.A.Bloy R.S.White
Kingsbury J.M.Knipe

'His dinner carefully wrapped in silken layers It sits motionless eyeing its exhausted prize'

KENDRA TABOR

Meerkats

Not merely cats,
They huddle together,
No African sun to warm them
Just the red lamp
Its warm glow a red sun on the rippled sand.
Eyes wide open
Scouts scanning the horizon
Still as rocks
Babies bob up and down
They chase and wrestle
And they scratch the sand for grubs
Hakuna Matata
Kings of their little sandy world.

In Memory of Bugless

She was cute
She was black
She was sanguine!

How did I know?
Because she loved me so!

For three months she stayed
Red grapes she craved.
Tickling her tummy
Made her feel funny.

How did i know?
Because her legs wriggled so!

Her brown furry chest
Was soft like a vest.
Her hard, cold shell
Was as shiny as a bell.

How did I know?
Because I cuddled her so!

A Rhino Beetle can be scary
But Bugless was a friend to me.

Tasmanian Devil's Plea

The end of my kind is near
Will we join our thylacine brothers?
Are your hands treacherous,
Or do you offer the gift of life?
But I fear it is too late for *me*.

Vast tumours spread rapidly
Across my deformed face.
A pool of dark blood surrounds my eyes
Weakening my sight.
My sense of smell fades under a malignant muzzle.

Once dressed in silky ebony
The radiance of my velvet coat
Has disappeared under death's cloak.
Before, I was as cuddly as a kitten
But now resemble a fierce, disfigured feral cat.

As I lie lifeless, in my den,
Clenched, curled in agony,
Hungry, unable to chase food,
Crying tears of blood,
My hope diminishes.

Slow moving, screeches and snarls are all I have
To protect me from my enemies.
You named me after evil,
But I am angel of the bushland
Eating the carrion that spreads disease.

It is not I who am the devil.
You slammed down the gavel
And ordered us a death sentence.
Anguish, grief and pain
Deepen my despair.

Isolated by my island refuge
I cannot escape the disease.
You talk of an ark that will save us all
Yet enclose me in armour of captivity.
I know my future

Sick and restricted on an island of grey,
My paradise, now a prison.
Nothing can save me,
But will you rescue my kind,
So another marsupial is not lost?

The Giraffe

In a big truck a giraffe stood just looking around.
When people saw they laughed and smiled.
As the truck moved on
More and more people
Became aware of this strange sight.
Some people questioned,
Some followed,
But the giraffe just stared
And looked around from a
Very great height.
Perhaps she was questioning where she was going,
Perhaps she was just curious about the curious.

Taronga Park

When I was young all the kids at school,
Were always going to the zoo,
Well I was brought up on a farm,
And never felt the need to.

I mean, we had animals coming out of our ears,
Chooks, ducks, pigs and lambs,
Horses, goats and steers.

Why would I want to visit a zoo?
In fact everything I'd seen,
Led me to believe that animals in captivity,
Was really rather mean.

I'd visualised a scene in my head,
Of animals scared and alone,
Stuck in cages, way too small,
A million miles from home.

I guess I was rather ignorant,
But then, I was rather young,
Not knowing endangered animals,
Were disappearing by the ton.

Elephants for their ivory,
The Tiger for its fur,
Monkeys left deserted,
Where once the forests were.

Whales are killed for blubber,
The Rhino for its horn,
Baby seals clubbed to death,
Their mothers left to mourn.

The Tasmanian Tiger – completely gone,
Extinct without a trace,
The Cheetah's numbers diminishing,
They can't outrun this race.

Now, I'm beginning to understand,
Exactly what they do,
When they place an endangered species,
Safely in a zoo.

People come to visit them,
And gain knowledge through this sight,
Of just how important it is for us,
To understand their plight.

Places like Taronga Park,
Are an essential part of life,
For animals at risk in the wild,
Where hunters and poachers are rife.

Monkey mayhem

We go to
    Dubbo Zoo
    for an
    early morning
    walk.

Past the rhino,
    by the giraffes

When,
    all of a sudden

Such a racket!

Few more steps,
    then

Monkey mayhem!

All swinging
    up high
    to a three-count
    beat.

Here comes food

Whoosh!

Here come dads

Take everything
    orange,
    scramble off.

All fuss

Leave greens
    for mums

Up they
    come.

Take
    what's left

Eat quietly,
    no fuss
    at
    all.

They really are
    like
    us.

Eastern Rosella Brothers

In the park
the unexpected
presence of such
graceful beauty, like
a bird that had ventured
through a rainbow,
arriving on the
other side with
all the vivid colours,
colours staining its
feathers. Soft plumage
like small, puffy clouds of
cotton, inquisitive and intelligent,
his crest of curiosity strikes the air,
high pitched songs bring music and
joy to the bushland; deep, ebony
eyes, wise and caring, hovering
momentarily, giving an ear-piercing
screech: Celebrating freedom,
before flying high above the
green blanket of trees
into the sunset
colours of
the evening
sky and
blending
as
one.

In the pet shop
His lonely brother flapping furiously
With nowhere to fly freely, a
Tormented captive in a grey prison.
Robbed so cruelly of his senses:
The smell of wafting eucalyptus,
The taste of fresh, flowering gum,
The sound of his faithful flock of friends,
The feel of rough bark under his claws,
The sight of miles of emerald canopies.

The
guilt
and the
obsession
unbearable; a
longing desire to
erase it from my
tormented memory.
Crying inside, and unable
to continue I purchase
the bird, to set it *free*,
so we will no longer
be Miserable

In His Mind's Eye

In his mind's eye,
The rosewood log was a man, the likeness of its maker.
The fallen gums were knives with deadly blades.
The silky-oak branch was an ancient game of mancala.
The twisted poplar was a walking stick.
The red-gum branch was a centrepiece for the table.
The gnarled bole of the red cedar was a doorstopper.

But the finest, most valued piece was
The sculpture made from Huon pine.

Two long, pointed ears like finely furred sentinels.
Two poorly-seeing eyes, round and dark.
A long, tapering snout; a naked, pink nose
That detects what the eyes do not.
A small furry body, silky blue and grey,
And a fold for the hidden pouch.
Two strong hind legs, with four sharp claws
That keep the long fur groomed.
Two front legs, with stout, curved claws
That powerfully dig and burrow.
This solitary creature stands alert,
Balanced on a black and white tail.
Endangered by man, extremely rare,
Shy digger of the Australian desert.

Most treasured of his carvings,
A Bilby in his eyes.

The Flibbitigibbit

The Flibbitigibbit
will flibble
and gibbit

He'll wiggle
and widgit
he'll niggle
and nibblet

The Flibbitigibbit
will flap
and flock

He'll moan
and meeeoooowww!
and scratch
and schlock!

The Flibbitigibbit
is nothing
but fur
he'll squiggle
and bubble
but never purr

He's an angry thing,
the Flibbitigibbit
he huffs
and puffs
like a Gibbitiflibbit!

10 Silly Zookeepers

10 silly zookeepers, tried to feed the lion,
One fell into the cage, and then there were 9

9 silly zookeepers, tried to catch the snake,
One tried to pick it up, and then there were 8

8 silly zookeepers, one went to heaven,
Because he smiled at the crocodile, and then there were 7

7 silly zookeepers, tried to chase the emu chicks,
Then the father came along, and then there were 6

6 silly zookeepers, approached a bee hive,
One tried to get some honey, and then there were 5

5 silly zookeepers, tried to sedate a boar,
One just ignored its horns, and then there were 4

4 silly zookeepers, saw gorillas eating fleas,
One thought he might join in, and then there were 3

3 silly zookeepers, knew the pelican flew,
So they tried to clip its wings, and then there were 2

2 silly zookeepers, tried to clean zebra dung,
The zebra started to stampede, and then there was 1

1 silly zookeeper, with one more thing to do,
Locked the gates and then realised, he couldn't get
back through!

Micio (Italian pet name for cat)

I see you first
a blur of ginger and white
leaping out of ruins
nonplussed yet eager to make a friend
When I beckon,
"Micio, vieni..."
you approach on nimble feet
It takes us no time
to establish a connection
only the time it takes you to
plough my shirt with your small claws
and butt my cheek with your nose
It is too hard to leave you
so defenceless
in a city so vast and full
of its own importance it has no time for you
Mum presses for us to move on
she is thinking about the rising heat
and more queues to join
But how can I return you to your
home of rubble and the indifference
of weary tourists?

Mum says to stop dramatising
but takes a photo for posterity
It isn't enough
I cry and swear
and will not see reason
I demand that we at least make inquiries
so for the next hour we find ourselves
in a nearby phone booth
trying to work out the Italian equivalent for the RSPCA
and whether the Australian Embassy can help
You could say mum is ropable now
exhausted and beyond sympathy
I have ruined the tour of the Colosseum for her
On our way back we search briefly for you
but without luck
I think I catch a glimpse of you
but you do not venture out this time
so there is nothing further to be done

Mum tries to be consoling
After all, you are not *lost*,
you are home...

I wish you knew I have framed the photo

White Cockatoo

A long time it has been
Since I have seen an escort
Draped in blinding white,
Welcoming the evening riches,
The heart lacquering honey-light.
A long time it has been
Since I have seen a fleet of white ships
Sailing through the hazy sunrise,
Catching glimpses of them between the trees.
A long time it has been,
Since I have heard your beckoning,
And unique ode to the bush.
A long time it has been
Since you have soared above me,
A flag of peace on elegant wings.
A long time it has been,
Since I have seen a White Cockatoo.

Spider

A web glistens in the moonlight
Hung from the corner of a sleeping child's room
A work of art, an intricate pattern for murder.
A home its hunting ground.

Long legs carry a small hairy body into hiding.
It waits.
A defenceless fly draws near, unaware of another's plans
In faded light, its eyes follow the fragile insect's every move
Carefully examining, ready for attacking.

His dinner carefully wrapped in silken layers
It sits motionless eyeing its exhausted prize
Exhilarated from its day's work
Up high, it stares down at an unfamiliar object
the light blue eye of a child,
watching.

Playing God

Today I bought a fish tank,
made of the clearest crystal glass.
It is round and shiny smooth
and light bounces off it in rainbows.

Pebbles drop in to line the base,
tinkling musically.
In goes the water, bubbly as a waterfall,
champagne-like. Then –

   Let there be light!
Fluorescent, coloured, and lots of it,
a liquid sphere glowing
in an otherwise dull and darkened room.

The best is saved for last –
the little creatures have arrived,
each in its very own plastic bag,
trying to break through

the invisible barriers,
gawking and goggling
open-mouthed, shocked
at each other's different features.

Finally released, they circle
around the glass tank,
wary at first, then
claiming territories proudly,

and crashing into the nothingness that is glass;
sooner or later they'll probably start killing each other,
but getting all the same type would have been boring.
Surely they'll find ways of getting along.

They amuse me, these fish,
indifferent to the outside world,
the world of ringing phones,
spilt coffee and piles of unread books;

If they are lucky, a shadow will come over their world
each day, raining down flakes of food,
and they'll come to the surface greedily gulping,
flicking their tails flippantly.

I wonder if they know me,
these fish in a bowl, that know nothing
of lakes or rivers or oceans.
Do they worry, and ponder

   where they came from
      or where they are going
         what they are
            and whether they actually exist?
And all of this
in a three-minute memory span.

Faith

They tell me
She is
A spy
From the insect world
And I believe them.
Because she won't pull the wings off
The beetles
That scuttle around the yard
Crawl up our sleeves
Shoot for our eyes
Land like ice cubes in our drinks.
They tell me
Her mother never makes her bed
And her father's been alongtimedead
But they couldn't prove nothing
In a court-a-law.
And her shoes that are a size too small
Won't let her run
From us at lunch
As we pull the wings off her beetles
And teachers avert their eyes or
Supervise,
They tell us
That she deserves it
And she believes them.

Ornithological Obstreperousness

Flamingos –
bimboesque birds,
fretful in their fluttering, feathered frames.
Riotous pink bodies skewered upon twiggy-stick legs –
yellow irises searching the crowd,
in this other Hollywood,
to see or be seen

preening, poising, prancing along the water-stage.
Thousands upon thousands,
a teeming, living mass parade.

Squawking and shrieking,
               "Look at me,
                  look at me!"
– Eardrums pierced by what the eyes cannot see.
Bowing heads as they swankily sip their
    delicious algaefied cocktail.
Every ditz dressed in the best pink-feather dress,
in the right crowd,
among the same people,
ready for the close-up.

Then come the paparazzi,
lions, leopards, cheetahs – jackals!

      And everyone knows it's time to exit the building.

(aq): reflections in Sydney Aquarium

I am underwater
but still apart
                (there are worlds behind that glass)
now
in the corridors of glass
the floor ripples
light drowns
background music
like water
the notes trickling down
liquid scales...

is there other music
played behind that glass?

                (glissandos of bubbles
                silent swishes of fins
                and the pulse
                of the currents)

schools of unblinking eyes
drift pass
unhurried...
is that angelfish
pondering?
why is that shark
so close?

                (have we come
                to see them,
                or do they come
                to see us?)

when I linger
too long
in the corridors of glass
I begin dissolving
my eyes swim
I start thinking
who

                                         (what)

am I
and will the scales to sprout
upon my back
you can pace
the corridors of glass
but you still can't go
where they go
you can't breathe water
you can only gaze
and wonder
what they're thinking

when I escaped
it was pouring with rain, drowning
the world

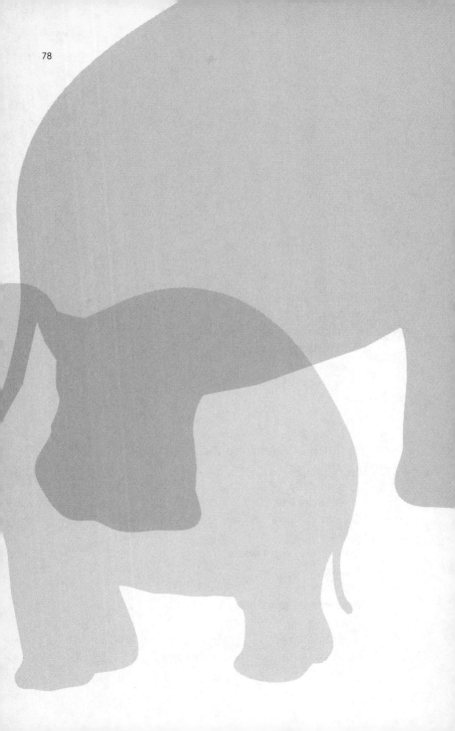

'The reflection of the
moon on the bay
means the soldier
crabs are out to play
in armed forces'

TASHINA CRAIGIE

Where I Live

Where I live, in Spring, the streets are lined with
humming yellow wattle, smelling of dusty old curtains
and thickly coated with hungry bees.
Pink and white, apple and cherry blossoms dance
about and blackberries begin their ruthless conquering
of other plants for the year.

Where I live, in Summer, bower bird – azure kleptomaniac,
builds his straw tower, decorates with a strange hoard
of blue treasure – pegs, straws, old toothbrushes, and
performs his deranged dance of love.
Hundreds of waratahs glow in the bush like Chinese
lanterns and an unseen army of snails emerge after rain.

Where I live, in Autumn, king parrots look like bright
tropical flowers and drop nuts from chestnut trees.
Maple tree leaves turn red, orange and gold
like fresh cooked cakes.
Leopard slugs look like writhing spotty sausages and
frolic in slow motion, basking in the mist.

Where I live, in Winter, I wake to a silent albino world.
Sun reflects off the snow like a mirror and I
see tiny perfect fox foot prints, flowers in the snow.

The Fossil

A piece of smashed car,
A tiny square of white glass.
On the road,
In the tar.
Like a fossil,
Of white bone.
Stuck,
In a tar pit.
What will they think?
When they dig it up,
Many years from now.

Move on

A mismatched melody echoes through humid air.
Birds fly all about their nests in the highest trees.
Snakes slither through undergrowth, lizards, under stones.
Peacocks dozing near trees rise to special dancing.
The ants scurry into their nests in formation.
Worms peep through the topsoil – they make weather
    forecasts.
There is silence in the forest.

Then it starts – a terrible torrent from the skies.
Water, followed by wind, swaying the strongest trees.
Meanwhile, the forest changes into an ocean.
Not a sea, an ocean. Completely overwhelmed,
Worms have retreated, deep down to the earth's centre.
The forest, too wet for the slimiest of eels.
"Will this ever end?" Most doubt it.

Birds wonder if their nests are strong enough for this.
The snakes and lizards are now climbers – up the trees.
The floor is higher – awash with muck and mire.
All doubt the survival of homes in the forest.
So sad, so helpless, surrounded by doom and gloom.
Fear is in the hearts of every forest creature.
"This will never end." – none doubt that.

By now some trees have been completely overwhelmed.
It has been raining hard from morning until night.
The owls peep out of their holes, and are scared as well.
Never has rain fallen like this in the forest.
The lightning strikes through. In turns,
One creature keeps watch, while the other sleeps.
"This will not end." – who *would* doubt that?

Now it is day. Finally the storm has ended.
Some still shiver. Their memories are flooding back.
None will complain in drought – they will remember this.
The water recedes quickly and all are happy.
Birds will not fly yet. Fear paralyses their wings.
"This will not end." – they remember their helplessness.
But echoes will not last. Move on.

As I sit

Once

I looked out

On a world where water was life and hope

Laughter, fun and games
Flowed through grassy fields
Smiles spread across my parents' faces
Dams overflowed
Corrugated tanks brimmed
As water trickled down the side
Magnificent marsupials with coats of chocolate
Leapt with glee, nibbling on lush pasture
Happy conversation at dinner
Food was abundant and varied
Satisfied sheep thrived on fertile terrain
Lambs frolicked, joyful and carefree
Wildflowers dotted the bushland
Like vivid stars in the sky
I remember picking a velvet flannel flower
And placing it between pages of my book

But now

As I look out

On a world marked by fears and tears

The sun's blazing rays burn the outback
While the vibrant sky never cries tears of rain
Gums stand on stiffened, sunbaked soil
Once majestic, but now stark
A cracked, clay dam bottom revealed by drought
Hollow water tanks echoing
Bare feet pattern dry dust that
Sifts through fingers like flour in a sieve
While parched kangaroos with joeys
Seek the canopy of a tree
Solemn sheep in powdery, ochre fields
Feed on shortened tufts of arid, yellow grass
"Fifty cents a sheep," the auctioneer cries
But a bullet is cheaper
Cheery wildflowers have vanished

As

I look inside

To a home wrapped in pain

Raised voices echo throughout corridors
Fear in my parents' eyes
Our farm under death's veil
Tension and furrowed brows at the dinner table
I go to bed hungry and invisible
Praying constantly for rain
My spirit crushed
Like the pressed flannel flower
I hold in my open book
I have withered and wilted
Like the beauty of its faded petals
Curling in agony in the corner of my bed
Waiting for the sound of pounding rain
And the taste of fresh water
With fading memories of my past world
Where water was plentiful

If only...

Of No Particular Blue

Long, lazy shadows lie splayed out
Across the mountain side,
Fingers out-reaching from every tree,
Silhouetted against the blazing, rising sun.
Currawong calls to announce the morning
From the top of a frayed mountain ash.
Platypus slithers into the river
With a ripple of sleek chocolate fur:
A porcelain-coated animal
Slides into the icy water, without so much as a splash.
Wrens emerge from their hiding
Wherever that may be,
And dart and play and twitter
On the protruding arms of the old, bony trees.
The biggest wren (of no particular blue is he),
Flies away over a golden field
Where the butter yellow and cream white-tipped flowers
Are moving ever so slightly,
One hundredth of an inch at a time,
Creating waves in a wondrous sea
As the dew crystallised rich green grass
Moves in harmony with the wind,
And bids the wren of no particular blue
Goodbye as he descends over a hilltop.

Hard Times

I've been around for a long, long time
Put down roots on this land of mine
But the last few months the heat and drought,
The hot cruel sun, it wears me out

I've been around for a long, long time
Like farmer John and his wife Caroline
We shared a picnic more than once
And the bush fire flames in the summer months

I've been around for a long, long time
But the heat and the air cling tight like a vine
I'm thirsty and dry and crave a drink
The river's so low not a stone would sink

I've been around for a long, long time
Saw John's dog, Jess, begin to whine
He used to lie on the grass all day
But the grass and the ground have turned to clay

I've been around for a long, long time
The sun beats down and I'm –
I'm weak, I'm dry, I've got a thirst
The sun beats down, no water's the worst

As John comes close and into view
He looks at me and sees right through
He has a radio with words that say
The drought continues, no rain today

He looks at me with pitiful eyes
Back and forth to the skies
"The dams are low for you, my friend
You're a great old tree, hard times never end"

Reflections

The reflection of the moon on the bay
means the marine life has slowed for the night.
You may still hear the waves crashing
on the beach and the rocks,
but you can't see the dolphins playing in the water,
or the tropical fish and corals brightening up the sea bed.

The reflection of the moon on the bay
means the sea birds are at rest
on their nests for the night,
but the penguins and mutton birds prefer the dark.

The reflection of the moon on the bay
means the soldier crabs are out to play in armed forces.
They scatter and scurry,
in such a hurry with no real place to go
except the rock pools, caves and dugouts in the sand.

The reflection of the moon on the bay
means the stingrays scavenge
around the shallows,
in and out of the mussel covered posts of the jetties.
You know they have been there
because at low tide
you can see their little and not so little
indents left in the sand of their body shape.

The reflection of the moon on the bay
means the Giant Bull Kelp forests
can sway calmly to the current
while the Great White Sharks silently
lurk within the underwater garden.

The reflection of the moon on the bay
means the jellyfish
which have lived in the ocean for millions of years,
silent, graceful and ghostly
move about their business.

The reflection of the moon on the bay
brings out the thousands of tiny eyes
of the shrimp and prawn
that come close to the shore for their evening meal.

The reflection of the moon on the bay means,
even though on the land we are at rest,
underwater never sleeps...

Borrowed Light

floating piano forte
fingers barely brush the keys
making unheard music
her head sways
to the orchestra
she's conducting

hands soar and rise,
striking with the unseen baton

with borrowed words
she'll tell us her story

cascading music
rippling through her body
she twists
and spins
to unheard music

and
with borrowed light
we'll see her...

she doesn't have to know
the key signature
she doesn't have to know
the meaning... the lyrics... the song

with borrowed words
she'll tell us her story
and
with borrowed light
we'll see her

she can't hear it
but she knows it's there
inside
she feels the trembling
of semi-quavers
the tumbling
of percussion
it's not sound anymore

she can't hear
what the singer says
and she'll never know the true meaning

but with borrowed words
she'll tell us her story
and
with borrowed light
we'll see her...

shivers
down her spine
she jumps, spinning… spinning...
then stops
her body twists, winds and spirals...
twirling, weaving, entwining the music with her hands
she forms her own melody...
no matter what the real lyrics say...

but with borrowed words
she'll tell us her story
and
with borrowed light
we'll see her...

her movements;
captivate
her expression;
entrances

– seeing is not always believing –
and it's no longer sound...

with borrowed words
she'll tell us her story
and
with borrowed light
we'll see her...

it doesn't matter
that we can't hear the music
with her, it's more than sound...

Dream

With a friend I trawled through a city of smog and glass
scrapers. Grey sprawled, stoked for incineration. I kept saying
I had to get to Canada. Canada wasn't a country. It was what
forest remained. I had to get there to breathe. I tried to nestle
in the centre of Canada,

sweet
music
green

so I could pretend it went on forever.
But the scrapers were there through the trees, however hard
I tried not to see them. They winked, tiny windows full-stop
mirrors in the sun.
In Canada there was a ring of the last, oldest trees. They had
faces, scars, rough brown bark. They had rings of years on
the inside and clear golden blood that caught things when
it ran, hardened to a jewel examined for history and in one
story even dinosaur DNA. Because there are no dinosaurs left.
And because we want to know the past. Under the leaves and
the smell of damp earth, in a patch of cool gloom, in the soft
scribbly places between plants, I breathe.
Some Aboriginal women come. They speak softly in my ear
secrets I don't remember. They point to a rusted relic, a metal
pedestal near the trees.

Secrets I don't remember would solve everything.

Ikebana

Strip away the dead leaves

and look! –

      one
    single leaf
    set against
     the air

    and the stem rising
    like the margin up a page
    and the lines of the twigs stretching out across.

The gaps are what let the readers see –
    Strip away the dead leaves,
        Ikebana poet!

treesong

i would have liked to think
that my ancestors were
the first spaceships
or
the sparks that burnt love
into the hearts of strangers.

but perhaps
i don't give trees
enough credit?

i can stand alone;
spend my hours practising.
but the stillness is something
completely separate – i often have trouble
resisting the winds
or
the urge to travel –
to lean while resting.

the browns and reds of autumn have,
of course,
been bred out
over generations

but i am,
without doubt,
a child of vines and oaks
of the deepest roots and
do not laugh:

there is blood in my veins that screams of reaching.

Afternoon on the Art Gallery Steps

All who passed here,

The children across the road
daubing expanses of pavement,
the girl whose eyelashes
drew hair-thin lines on her cheek,
the man under the trees,
who melted into a lattice
of sun and leaves, all

have walked into this sketchbook.

It was a time when shadows grew
and cast their people. One I remember,
stretching out in a young woman's wake;
as I shaded the drawn-out darkness,
the sun came down and balanced

on her forehead, then was gone.

Evening
deepened, the dusk's
soft finger smudged
the edges of things

till I could no longer
see the page before me.

Only the blackest
charcoal strokes, the bats,
remained.

INDEX OF PRIZE-WINNING POEMS

JUNIOR DIVISION

INTERMEDIATE DIVISION

SENIOR DIVISION

INDEX OF AUTHORS

THE TARONGA FOUNDATION POETRY PRIZE

In 2003, The Taronga Foundation and Poetry Australia Foundation banded together with bestselling author Bradley Trevor Greive to create the Taronga Foundation Poetry Prize – Australia's leading youth poetry competition.

The aims of the prize are to instil a love of poetry and the environment, and to nurture, support and provide publishing opportunities for young creative talent.

In 2004, the Taronga Foundation Poetry prize awarded over $20,000 in prizes, including $9,000 in cash prizes. This year, $28,000 worth of prizes were on offer, including cash, book vouchers, books, passes to Australia's premier zoos and eco-venues, trophies, certificates and stickers. The very best entries each year are published by Random House Australia in *Poems by Young Australians.*

Poems may be on any subject, but a special $3,000 (plus trophy and prizes) Wildlife Prize is awarded for the most outstanding poem across all divisions, dealing with issues of wildlife conservation and the environment. Prize categories for 2005 were:

- Senior: 16 to 19 years inclusive. Prizes offered for national ($2000, trophy plus prizes) and state/territory winners ($300, trophy plus prizes).
- Intermediate: 12 to 15 years inclusive. Prizes offered for national ($1000, trophy plus prizes) and state/territory winners ($200, trophy plus prizes).
- Junior: 11 years and under. Prizes offered for national ($1000, trophy plus prizes) and state/territory winners ($200, trophy plus prizes).

A new inclusion is the class/group poem, which is a special prize category for the best poem written by a class or group of poets 15 years and under; $3000 in book vouchers is on offer to this category.

Every poet who submits an entry receives a prize – a certificate and sticker, and free entry to Taronga Zoo or the participating zoo or eco-venue in their state/territory on the day of the award ceremony and anthology launch in October of that year. (See the Taronga Foundation Poetry Prize Conservation Partners in the following pages for details of participating zoos/eco-venues.)

Entries open for the 2006 Taronga Foundation Poetry Prize on 1 October 2005. Entry forms are available for download on www.btgstudios.com/poetryprize.html or www.tarongafoundation.org or by contacting the Prize Coordinator Nerida Robinson on phone (02) 4464 3331 or email tfpp@btgstudios.com

ABOUT THE TARONGA FOUNDATION

Nature is our most valuable asset, yet every day the survival of animal and plant species and their environment are threatened.

The best zoos around the world have realised their role in this struggle. Taronga Zoo and Western Plains Zoo are among them, passionately committed to the conservation of our environment.

Taronga Zoo and Western Plains Zoo see it as their role to connect people to nature in a meaningful way. They do this by engaging with the 1.5 million people who tour the zoos, the 110,000 school children who attend the education programs, and the 30,000 people visited by the Zoomobile every year. These visits lead to a better understanding of wildlife and therefore of its conservation and preservation.

But Taronga and Western Plains want to take their commitment to conservation further and have developed a plan to do so. The Master Plan ensures that Taronga and Western Plains Zoos maintain conservation as a priority through research, breeding and education. This commitment takes these zoos all around the world, undertaking conservation and research projects, from rhino programs in Zimbabwe to seals in Antarctica.

The Plan also includes the new Asian Elephant Rainforest – one of the world's most important conservation and education projects and our theme for the 2005 Taronga Foundation Poetry Prize. This Asian Elephant Rainforest will allow visitors to walk through a simulated Asian village, with aviaries and underwater viewing, providing close encounters with the many endangered animals living here – including Asian elephants and one of only seven breeding pairs of Silvery Gibbons in world zoos.

African ecologist, Baba Dioum once famously said – 'In the end, we will conserve only what we love, we will love only what we understand, and we will understand only what we are taught'.

The Taronga Foundation was established to put this philosophy into action – to create a better future for wildlife and our children. Half of the proceeds of the sale of this anthology go to the Taronga Foundation. Donations are tax deductible and for every dollar donated, the NSW government gives three more. For more information, you can contact the Taronga Foundation by phone (02) 9978 4616 or visit www.tarongafoundation.org

2005 TARONGA FOUNDATION POETRY PRIZE OFFICE HOLDERS

BRADLEY TREVOR GREIVE – CHAIRMAN

Bradley Trevor Greive (BTG) was born in Australia's untamed island state of Tasmania in 1970, although he spent most of his childhood living in Scotland, England, Wales, Hong Kong and Singapore. After returning to Australia, BTG graduated from the Royal Military College and served as a paratroop platoon commander in the Australian army. Since leaving the military to seek creative misadventure, BTG has become one of Australia's most successful authors. His books have been published in more than forty countries and he has numerous international bestsellers to his credit, including *Priceless; The Vanishing Beauty of a Fragile Planet, The Meaning of Life, Tomorrow* and *The Blue Day Book*, which received the 2000 Australian Book of the Year Award. Bradley Trevor Greive is a Governor of the Taronga Foundation and supports wildlife conservation projects throughout the world.

RON PRETTY, AM – DIRECTOR

Ron Pretty has been a published poet for more than thirty years, receiving an AM for services to Australian literature in 2002. He has published four books of poetry, including *Of the Stone: New and Selected Poems* and *Creating Poetry*. He was editor of the literary/arts magazine *SCARP* and has taught writing in schools, universities and community groups throughout Australia, North America, England and Austria. He is currently Director of Five Islands Press, the leading publisher of contemporary Australian poetry, and with John Millett, has established the Poetry Australia Foundation, a community-based, non-profit organisation that promotes the writing, reading, reviewing and promotion of poetry in this country. He is managing editor of *Blue Dog: Australian Poetry*, the first edition of which was published in June 2002.

DR BROOK EMERY – CHIEF JUDGE

A former English and History teacher, Brook Emery has won many awards for his poetry, including the Bruce Dawe Award and the Newcastle Poetry Prize. His collection *and dug my fingers in the sand* won the Judith Wright Calanthe Award and was shortlisted for the NSW Premier's Award. His most recent book, *Misplaced Heart* (Five Islands Press, 2003) was shortlisted for the 2004 NSW Premier's Award. Brook has a PhD in Literature from the University of Newcastle and is Chairperson of the Poets Union.

DEB WESTBURY – JUDGE

Deb Westbury has worked as a teacher of writing in schools and universities and has published four books of poetry. Her most recent book, *Flying Blind*, was published by Brandl & Schlesinger in 2002, and an earlier book, *Mouth to Mouth*, is a chosen text for the NSW Higher School Certificate course.

DR KERRY WHITE – JUDGE

Dr Kerry White is a bibliographer, writer and reviewer. She is the author of *Australian Children's Books: a Bibliography* (2 volumes), and of *Australian Children's Fiction: the Subject Guide* (2 volumes). She is the major contributor to *The Source*, a web-based guide to children's books and poetry.

THE TARONGA FOUNDATION POETRY PRIZE CONSERVATION PARTNERS

The National Zoo and Aquarium

The National Zoo and Aquarium in Canberra is Australia's only combined zoo and aquarium, a place where visitors can experience exotic and native animals, birds and reptiles alongside sharks, ocean and freshwater fish.

The Zoo boasts the largest collection of big cats in Australia and is renowned for its interactive visitor experiences, ranging from handfeeding of big cats and bears to playing with cheetahs or accompanying keepers on their daily rounds.

The Zoo is actively committed to wildlife conservation through its involvement in endangered species breeding programs. For more information: www.zooquarium.com.au or phone (02) 6287 8400.

Zoos Victoria

Zoos Victoria (Melbourne Zoo, Healesville Sanctuary and Werribee Open Range Zoo) is committed to inspiring, educating and empowering people to engage with wildlife and help conserve the natural world.

This commitment is evident in some of the newest zoo experiences. At Healesville, visitors can connect with injured wildlife; at Werribee, they can consider how to live alongside animals at Hippo River; and at Melbourne, they can investigate the intelligence of orang-utans.

The zoos have a particular focus on student learning and discovery. Together, they deliver a contextual learning experience where students and visitors have the opportunity to connect with animals in their natural settings.   These unique learning experiences support the Victorian Essential Learning Standards and the post-compulsory frameworks (VCE, etc).

For more information: www.zoo.org.au or phone (03) 9285 9300.

Adelaide Zoo

Adelaide Zoo, with its 120-year history and rich architectural heritage, boasts state of the art breeding and animal management programs.

The Zoo's philosophy and commitment to conservation and education is encapsulated in its latest exhibit, IMMERSION The South East Asian Rainforest. Stage Two of this ambitious project will be completed in late 2005.

The exhibit creates open, natural habitats for the Zoo's Sumatran tigers and orang-utans (as well as other new species), at the same time providing unprecedented opportunities for visitor interaction, as well as improved wildlife breeding facilities.

For more information: www.adelaidezoo.com.au or phone (08) 8267 3255.

Perth Zoo

Perth Zoo has a vision of a world in which people's eyes are open to nature. By providing an engaging visitor experience, the Zoo endeavours to positively impact on community attitudes to wildlife preservation.

The new African Painted Dog exhibit is one such example. The exhibit recreates the sights and sounds of the African savannah, providing a unique opportunity to see these endangered animals in something close to their natural environment. The Zoo's breeding program has also been a major success, with the birth of six puppies in April this year.

A range of learning materials has been specially developed to support the African savannah experience, aimed at students from kindergarten to Year 12.

For more information: visit www.perthzoo.wa.gov.au or phone (08) 9474 0365.

Territory Wildlife Park

Territory Wildlife Park enables visitors to immerse themselves in the Top End experience. Exhibits such as the Aquarium, Nocturnal House, Reptiles, Arthropods and Bird Aviaries are set amidst monsoon rainforest, natural springs, paperbark wetlands and billabongs connected by extensive walking trails.

The Park prides itself on providing visitors with an opportunity to get close to animals that are often difficult to see in the wild. In particular, its daily shows and special programs allow visitors to enjoy personal encounters with both the animals and their keepers.

For more information: www.territorywildlifepark.com.au or phone (08) 8988 7200.

Australia Zoo

The home of the Crocodile Hunter, Steve Irwin, is also home to an amazing array of native and exotic animals and a committed team of wildlife conservationists.

Aside from providing visitors with an 'up close and personal experience' of everything from Australian saltwater crocodiles to elephants, the Zoo is actively engaged in breeding programs for a variety of endangered species and provides a focus for a range of wildlife and habitat conservation programs. An example of this focus is the Zoo's latest exhibit, Tiger Temple, home to five tigers and four cheetahs.

The Zoo also boasts expansive grounds and facilities, including the 5,000 seat Animal Planet Crocoseum where visitors enjoy a bird's-eye view of live shows featuring snakes, tigers, birds and crocodiles.

For more information: www.crocodilehunter.com or phone (07) 5436 2000.

Dismal Swamp

North-west Tasmania's newest ecotourism attraction allows visitors to discover an ancient landscape.

Dismal Swamp was created over the millennia by the slow dissolution by water of the sinkhole's dolomite bedrock. The sinkhole is now home to many species of plants and animals that have adapted to its shadowy, moist environment.

On the swamp floor, maze-like paths take visitors through several microclimates featuring manfern groves, paperbarks, myrtles and blackwoods. This rich plant life is matched by an array of birds and other swamp creatures, such as burrowing crayfish, spotted-tail quolls and pademelons.

For more information: www.tasforestrytourism.com.au or phone (03) 6456 7199.

ABOUT THE POETRY
AUSTRALIA FOUNDATION

The Poetry Australia Foundation, now based at the University of Melbourne, has been established to promote the enjoyment of poetry and the writing, reading, reviewing and distribution of poetry in all its forms. The Poetry Australia Foundation has been incorporated as a not-for-profit, community-based organisation. All donations to the Foundation over $2.00 are tax-deductible. The activities of the Foundation include:

- supporting the administration of the Taronga Foundation Poetry Prize and judging the entries
- publishing the poetry magazine *Blue Dog: Australian Poetry* and running the BTG-Blue Dog Poetry Reviewing Competition
- running poetry workshops, online workshops, readings, seminars and conferences
- supporting the work of Five Islands Press, which publishes only poetry. In turn, any profits made by Five Islands Press will be returned to support the work of the Foundation
- conducting readings by local, national and international poets
- exploring the possibilities of poetry at all levels of education
- establishing a library of Australian poetry
- supporting the work of other publishers of poetry through the distribution of an annual catalogue of Australian poetry.

One of the beliefs underpinning the work of the Foundation is that many more people would read and enjoy poetry if only they could find it. So one of the aims of the Foundation is to make it easier for people to find the poetry that is available, and to find the poetry they like. Another aim is to support poets of all ages in the writing, revising, publication and distribution of their work.

For further information, contact Ron Pretty on 03 8344 8713 or email rpretty@unimelb.edu.au

Our webpage is at http://www.sca.unimelb.edu.au/paf/index.html